Punished By The Doms

Annika Rhyder

Published by Annika Rhyder, 2018.

PUNISHED BY THE DOMS

Annika Rhyder

Blurb

Jessa

I've always been too curious, so I sneak downstairs to spy on my employers' party. What's was the harm? Their children are upstairs asleep, and I just want a little peek. Except I don't expect to find my bosses watching a BDSM scene with a woman and two men. Dante and Patrick are gay, right? So why are they watching a woman dominate her lovers? And why do they think spanking me is the perfect punishment for my infraction? Most of all, if they're gay, why are they touching me so sensually?

Patrick

She thinks we're gay, but she couldn't be more wrong. After losing our wife two years ago, we've sworn off taking on a long-term sub, but when I find out she's a virgin everywhere, I can't hold back. Dante's my oldest friend and shares my tastes, so I know he feels the same way. We're only supposed to spank her for breaking our rules, but when I touch her, I can't stop.

Dante

I've tried pretending I didn't want to dominate the hot nanny, but I'm done with the pretense. She's spread out before us, and I can't help a taste. The problem is, she's addictive, and one taste makes me want another and another. She's too young and inexperienced for our games, but that doesn't matter. Nothing matters except Jessa's sweet submission. I know we said never again, but I'm having second thoughts about that...

WORKING AS A PART-TIME nanny for Dante Cavello and Patrick Shelley is a dream job for college student Jessa Wyler. She adores the kids almost as much as their dads. She assumes they're a gay couple raising their children, but she couldn't be more wrong. When her curiosity gets the best of her, they catch her spying on their BDSM party. She has to be punished for the infraction with a bare-bottom spanking that escalates to more. They soon discover she's a virgin in every way, and they're going to take care of that—together, at the same time!

The desire between the three of them is explosive, but the widowers don't want a serious commitment, and the more she submits to them, the more she wants everything, not just a short fling. Being punished by the doms might lead to more than spankings and incredible pleasure. It could break her heart.

If you like two older alpha men dominating their virgin nanny, a taste of BDSM, and sexy times, pick up this novella for steamy reading.

This is a MFM ménage romance. It's about 25,000 words and includes a one-chapter excerpt for another Annika Rhyder title at the end.

Chapter One

Jessa

Curiosity killed the cat. Everyone knew that, but I didn't pay any attention to it. I was burning with curiosity to find out what Dante Cavello and Patrick Shelley were doing on the bottom floor of their apartment, from where they had banned me and the kids for the evening.

I babysat for the men frequently, but could only think of two other occasions where they had explicitly told me I couldn't come downstairs. Both times, I'd been curious, but the kids had trouble sleeping, and I hadn't had the chance to indulge my inquisitiveness.

Tonight was different. Sam and Tam had fallen asleep about twenty minutes ago, and their little sister Cori wasn't far behind. I'd spent the last ten minutes sitting on the comfortable couch in the upstairs family room of their Manhattan apartment trying to talk myself out of snooping.

I was losing the argument with myself. After all, it wasn't exactly like snooping. I wasn't going to be prowling through their drawers and invading their private things. I just wanted to know what was going on downstairs.

I'd heard the doorbell ring a few times, but the kids and I had been upstairs, and I hadn't had a chance to even sneak a peek at their guests. I assumed they were having some kind of party, which was probably why I wasn't allowed down there either. I was only nineteen, so I couldn't legally drink. That, and I was there to watch the kids, not participate in their parties. They probably thought *I* was a kid, and I guessed I was to both of them.

Dante and Patrick were both handsome and mature, and it didn't hurt that they were loaded. That wasn't important to me, but I knew it must sway quite a few women their direction. I knew they were in their thirties, but not exact ages. Seeing how close they were, I was sure they were very much in love, and they were raising a family together too. They wouldn't see the nineteen-year-old babysitter as anything but a kid, so no wonder they hadn't invited me.

I could be overly sensitive, but I was trying to fight against the tendency as I reminded myself sternly that I was their employee, not their friend. Besides, someone had to be with the kids.

But they were all three sleeping peacefully, with the twins curled up in the big full bed they shared, since they hadn't yet learned to sleep apart, and adorable Cori—who had Dante's thick black hair in a head full of curls—slept in her toddler bed. Almost two, she hadn't quite outgrown it yet. The kids were fine, and I could always take the baby monitor with me.

It was still a bad idea, but I had convinced myself just to take a quick peek and satisfy my curiosity. My mom would chastise me for the decision and remind me that being inquisitive wasn't good, but she wasn't there to be a stifling presence to quell my natural nosiness.

I scooped up the baby monitor, which was a sophisticated machine capable of monitoring the twins' room and Cori's, and padded down the hallway on bare feet. The gleaming marble should've been cold under my feet, but this was a luxury apartment, so there were warmers built into the flooring. I was toasty warm, and leaving behind my shoes would allow me to move more silently.

I had a fizzy feeling in my stomach as I crept down the stairs. It was mingled excitement and fear. I knew I was being naughty, but the experience itself was enjoyable, even if there was the fear of getting caught.

I'd expected music or something, since it was a party, but there was no obvious activity on the bottom floor, at least not in the great room or the other family room farther down the hall.

That left just one possibility, unless they were having some kind of cooking party and had gathered in the restaurant-worthy kitchen. They had to be in the large study they shared. It seemed like an odd place for a party, but as I crept closer, I heard the low hum of voices muffled by the thick door.

Cautiously, I turned the knob and waited to see if it would squeak. Of course it didn't, because everything in the Cavello–Shelley household functioned perfectly, as was expected for the amount of money they spent. Except me at the moment. I was "malfunctioning" by not obeying their strict instructions to stay upstairs.

I was surprised when I opened the office and found they weren't there either. That wasn't the biggest surprise of the evening. One of the walls was open in a secret entrance just like out of an old *Scooby Doo* episode.

I bit my lip, contemplating if I should really cross the office and explore, or if I should just forget the whole idea and hurry back upstairs. Still, I had come all this way, and I'd never been through a secret entrance before.

Tiptoeing quietly across the floor, though I probably didn't need to bother since the thick carpet would absorb the footsteps of a herd of elephants without a sound, I reached the entrance. It was open halfway, so I peeked in, but didn't step through.

I froze in shock at the sight before me, at first uncertain what I was seeing. There was a stern-looking woman in a black vinyl catsuit holding a whip. Two men knelt at her feet, and they were both licking her boots. I shuddered in disgust at the idea and clamped a hand over my mouth when I realized I'd let out a small gasp.

It was the gasp that revealed me, I guessed, because Dante stiffened and turned to face me. Patrick stood beside him, along with a few others, who appeared to be observing whatever drama was happening in the center of the room.

I held my breath when Dante scowled at me before turning to nudge Patrick. When both sets of eyes focused on me—one vivid blue, and one such a deep brown as to be almost black, and both filled with anger—I shivered.

I backed away quickly, turning to run from the office. I dared hope they would just ignore my intrusion, but when Dante called my name a moment later, I froze at the doorway. I didn't look back at him, but I clutched the doorjamb for support as I waited for him to lecture me.

"Return upstairs and wait there. Don't even think about leaving, Jessa." He spoke calmly, and without any obvious anger, but with such a strong note of authority I couldn't even think of questioning the command.

I started moving again, abandoning subtlety in my haste to hurry upstairs. I threw myself on the couch I'd abandoned only a few minutes before and hugged a throw pillow to my chest as I fretted.

At first, my thoughts were wholly consumed by what Dante and Patrick might do to me. They were surely going to fire me, which really sucked. I didn't want go back to my old job working at a hot dog stand.

In fact, that was how I'd met the family, having served their Saturday hot dogs to them for several weeks in a row. The boys must have really liked me, because a few weeks after I'd met the family, Dante and Patrick asked if I'd like to be their part-time nanny. The hours were manageable with my class load, and it was only a short subway ride from their apartment to the one I shared with my mom and back again. The pay was a heck of a lot better to, and it had been an ideal situation. I adored the kids, and I secretly adored the men as well, but was certain they had eyes only for each other.

What was going on downstairs then? I wasn't completely naïve. I might be a virgin, but I knew enough about BDSM to infer that was what I witnessed. I shuddered with revulsion for a moment, remembering the bootlickers, but couldn't help imagining myself in the position of power like the woman. There was a tantalizing naughtiness to the idea, though I was certain I wouldn't be very good at telling people under me what to do. What do they call those? Subordinates? No, that didn't sound right.

I reached for my tablet and quickly looked it up, discovering the proper terms. I was certain I wasn't the dominatrix type the more I read, and the idea of being someone's slave didn't sit well with me. I couldn't deny there was a spark of curiosity about the submissive part though. That sounded like it could be fun with the right partner.

Or partners. I stared at a woman on the small screen for a moment, imagining what it was like to be the one on my knees, with my hands cuffed behind my back, and a leather bit between my teeth. It was a disconcerting thought, but I was shocked by how arousing I found the idea as well. My nipples hardened, and my panties were damp in no time.

I cleared my throat and quickly exited out of the site, having temporarily appeased my curiosity. I was still surprised to find out Dante and Patrick were into that sort of thing though. And if they were, I would've expected it to be a gathering of all men, but there had been about an equal number of women as well.

I was intrigued by what was going down on downstairs, but was certain I'd never have further information. If by some chance they just gave me a stern talking-to and didn't fire me, I'd never have the nerve to bring up what I'd seen. If they fired me, I wouldn't have a chance either, because I'd be gone. I didn't live with the family, but I spent some nights there—enough that I had my own drawer of things stashed in the guest room. The thought of not returning sent a pang through my chest. I had really screwed up badly, and I just hoped they could forgive me.

After what felt like an interminable wait, I heard their footsteps on the steps and held my breath as I waited for them to enter the family room. It didn't take them long, though the last few seconds were like an eternity as I waited to discover if they would fire me. I clenched my hands together as they entered, and their stern expressions sent a jolt of fear through me. I stared at them for a moment, but neither spoke. They stood with their arms crossed over their chests, both giving me looks that I wouldn't call angry, but certainly weren't pleased either.

"I'm so sorry. I shouldn't have done it, I just got curious, but I know was wrong. Please—"

"Enough," said Patrick in the firmest voice I'd ever heard him use, especially directed toward me. "Be silent."

I didn't appreciate his tone, or the command, but I wasn't able to resist following it. I stopped speaking and stared at my hands in my lap as I waited to see what they would say.

"Look at us," said Dante.

I lifted my head slowly, looking in their general vicinity, but unable to meet either set of eyes focused on me.

"We gave you very clear instructions, but you didn't comply. You need to be punished for that."

My gaze swung to Patrick when he spoke those words, and I eyed him with confusion. "Punished? Do you mean fired? I'm really sorry—"

"Don't speak without permission," barked Dante. He practically radiated power and authority as he walked over to me.

I was finding it less difficult to imagine either one of them being involved in the BDSM scene now, but was still perplexed by it appearing to be mixed gender. "Sorry." I barely whispered the word, holding my breath to see if he would chastise me again.

"When the children don't listen, there are consequences. They lose privileges, but we can't very well do that with you."

I looked up hopefully at Dante and nodded my agreement with his words. I still didn't speak though. Maybe they weren't going to pay me for tonight. If I got to keep the job, I was okay with that.

"We talked it over, and we decided what you need is a spanking."

My gaze swung to Patrick, and I laughed nervously. "That's funny." It wasn't exactly funny though. The joke—and it had to be a joke—might've been intended to lighten the mood, but it just sent a slow trickle of heat flicking along my nerve endings. I supposed I should be afraid at the thought, but I was more intrigued than frightened by the idea of either one of them spanking me. They were joking though. They had to be.

Chapter Two

Patrick

She thought we were joking. That made me chuckle, but it was a dark sound. I was looking forward to seeing her reaction when she realized we weren't kidding. Of course, we wouldn't force her to submit to a spanking, but she had to pay for her infraction of the rules. It was a basic fact of life, though she'd been a good girl up to this point and had given us no reason to discipline her.

I wouldn't pretend like I hadn't been a little excited to see her in the doorway, spying on the scene we were hosting. It had lingered in the back of my mind that I'd like to spank her nicely rounded ass on more than one occasion, and now I had a chance. If she agreed.

"Not just a spanking," said Dante. "Bare-assed so you actually feel it."

I nodded, forcing my expression to be stern as we loomed over her.

She frowned as it started to sink in that we weren't kidding. "You're joking, right?"

I shook my head slowly. "No. That's your punishment."

She arched a brow. "I don't think that sort of thing is legal."

"It's perfectly legal as long as everyone involved consents," I said. I sounded almost bored. I was anything but though, already keyed up from almost an hour of anticipating this moment, combined with the excitement of soon smacking that sweet ass.

"But I didn't consent."

"You did agree to follow our rules when we first hired you," said Dante. "You broke one tonight, and this is the consequence of doing so. You can refuse, but I'm afraid we might not be able to trust you after this evening. You need to earn a second chance."

Her eyes were big now, and she looked afraid, but her expression revealed something else. There was a gleam of interest in her eyes, and her breathing quickened. She was definitely intrigued by the idea, if not excited. At least not yet.

"Will you fire me if I don't?"

We shared a look, having already reached a consensus, but I assumed Dante wanted to be sure I hadn't changed my mind, and I needed to the same reassurance from him. We both nodded in unison.

"I'm afraid so. Our kids love you, and you're great with them, but we have to be able to trust you."

She was frowning, and there was a bead of perspiration on her brow. "How does letting you spank me rebuild trust?"

"It shows you're willing to take responsibility for your actions, and we hope it deters you from making the same mistake again." Dante spoke quietly, and his calm assurance seemed to help Jessa past a moment of real fear.

She trembled for a moment before taking a deep breath. "Okay, I guess. I mean, it makes sense, since you guys are into all that." Her face was bright red as she finished speaking, and her lips—outlined in some kind of cherry-red gloss that would taste gross, but would leave an impressive ring on my cock—trembled independently for a moment before she firmed them. With what looked like a decisive nod of her head, she squared her shoulders and stood up. "All right, I'm ready. How do we do this?"

"Pull down your pants and underwear." My dick throbbed at the thought.

She frowned again. "I thought you were just kidding about the bare-bottom thing."

Dante laughed. "I don't joke when it comes to discipline, pet." He made a twirling motion with his fingers, and Jessa complied by turning around.

She was trembling again, but not as noticeably as before. Her hands went to her waistband, but she seemed incapable of pulling down her pants.

I stepped forward and put my hands over hers to help her pull down the yoga pants to her knees. "Bend over the arm of the couch with your ass in the air."

She made a little moaning sound, and it was full of fear, but that wasn't all she was feeling. I could tell a moment later when she bent over in the position I'd instructed. Her pussy was shiny with the cream slowly leaking from her. The scent of her arousal wafted to my nose, and I inhaled deeply to savor it.

My cocked twitched in my pants, and I stepped forward eagerly. We hadn't discussed who would spank her first, but Dante took a step back, likely sensing my urgency. We were in sync that way.

I cupped her luscious globes for just a moment, allowing a tantalizing second to test their weight and contours. I was definitely an ass man.

I wanted to get my fingers inside her cunt and test her wetness, but punishment had to come before pleasure. I brought back my hand and clapped it firmly against her bare buttocks, wishing I had a flogger instead.

She moaned at the first spank, but it was difficult to tell if she was protesting or enjoying. Either way, she didn't ask me to stop, so I spanked her again. This time, it was harder, as was the next and the next. I wanted to keep smacking her ass until it was bright red, but Dante wanted a turn as well, and the poor girl had to be able to stand and walk the next day. Besides, she wasn't ours to mark. This was already pushing the bounds, but I still couldn't resist one last swat before I rubbed her cheeks for a moment.

She moaned, and her butt pressed firmly against my hand, which made me laugh. Her juices coated my hand as I pulled away, revealing how aroused she was by her punishment.

Dante stepped forward then, and his hands were larger than mine. He didn't bother with cupping her ass first to explore its contours. He simply brought back his hand and hit her firmly.

She cried out and jerked forward, obviously stunned by the intensity of his spanking. She looked over her shoulder, and her lips trembled. There was fear in her eyes, but that subtle hint of curiosity and desire also remained. She licked her lips when her gaze met mine, and she seemed to be poised on the verge of saying something, but just bit her lip when he smacked her again.

"I wish I had my paddle," said Dante with a laugh in my direction.

"I was just thinking about a flogger." I'd start out with the softest and easiest one for her, with its supple leather strands that would caress her skin even as it bit hard enough to leave faint red marks. Then we'd eventually work up to something that would leave proof of domination on her skin that would last longer than a few seconds.

My cock was pressing insistently against the zipper of my slacks at the moment, and I palmed the length for a moment, though it did nothing to tame the raging hard-on.

Dante kept his spanking brief, but he had made up for it with intensity. I was certain three or four spanks from him was equivalent to far longer punishment from just about any other Dom. Now, he turned from stern to tender as he stroked her butt, squeezing her pink cheeks gently between both of his hands.

I moaned as his thumb slid up the crack of her ass, though he didn't allow himself the temptation of pressing in on her puckered rosette to see if it would yield to him. I wouldn't have been able to resist, but Dante wasn't as ass-oriented as I was.

His digits moved down again, and this time he didn't stop. Two of his fingers slipped out of sight as they went between her thighs, and I envied my best friend for being the first one to dip inside her silken heat.

"How is she?" My voice sounded raspy.

"Wet as fuck and clearly enjoying her punishment." He clicked his tongue. "I'm not sure it's punishment if you get turned on like this. I'm not convinced you've learned your lesson yet, pet."

She was shaking her head frantically, but still hadn't spoken. As Dante's hand started to move, she moaned and pressed down against him.

I couldn't hold back any longer, and I crossed the room to join them. I slid my hands between her thighs, feeling for Dante's fingers. They were focused on rubbing her clit, so I dipped into her opening, but not too far. I suspected our sweet part-time nanny was still a virgin.

My shaft tightened even further at the thought of being the first one to claim her holes. I couldn't restrain myself and slid my fingers backward, pressing one against the stubborn ring of muscle in her ass.

She clenched up tighter than Fort Knox, and there was an ambiguous sound coming from her. I couldn't tell if she was excited, afraid, or both. I hesitated, waiting for her to tell me no, but she didn't. She remained silent, still pressing insistently against Dante's hand as he continued fingering her clit.

When her ass relaxed, I took advantage of the moment to press my finger inside her. It went in slowly, and then easily as her muscles yielded to the intrusion. She whimpered, but it was a sound of ecstasy rather than rejection.

"She's so wet," said Dante. "Bet she tastes delicious."

It was my turn to moan at the idea, and I found myself unable to speak for a moment. Instead, I settled for wiggling my finger in her ass and making her whimper in protest even as she pressed harder against my hand. I was pretty sure Jessa liked it, even though she didn't want to like it.

"She's tight." Dante seemed to have trouble pushing the words through gritted teeth. From the position of his hand, and my viewpoint, I could see he'd pulled away from her clit and put a finger inside her. A moment later, he started rubbing her clit again while sliding his thumb in and out of her hole. There was a squelching sound that was sexy as fuck, because it told me just how wet she was, and more than a drop of pre-cum dripped from my dick. I longed to pull down my pants and slide inside her, but it was too soon for that. Besides, this was about punishment.

Bullshit. I was pretty sure we had veered away from punishment sometime between starting the endeavor and me ending up with my finger in her ass and Dante's inside her pussy.

"She's about to come." A bead of sweat was visible on Dante's brow. "I can feel her clenching around me."

I brought up my other hand, moving between her legs to slide a finger alongside Dante's as her sheath tightened and convulsed around us. Jessa let out a low moaning sound as she bucked her hips and pressed down against our fingers. Her ass muscles clenched tightly enough that I couldn't pull out my finger for a moment, but I didn't want to. I would've liked to stay inside her hot body all day, though I would rather have my dick than my fingers inside her.

"Good girl. The punishment's over." Dante was more levelheaded in the moment.

I was still reeling from her slick walls clamping around my digits as my finger rubbed against Dante's thumb while we fingered her to completion. It wasn't quite as good as the real thing, but it had been pretty earthshaking in its own right.

She didn't look at either one of us as she pulled up her pants and grabbed her things. Her expression revealed how overwhelmed she was by everything. I hated to let her run out into the night, but I figured she wouldn't be receptive to either one of us offering her help at the moment. It had been an intense first experience for her, and she needed time to process what had happened.

Chapter Three

Dante

I watched her go, wishing I could call her back and entice her to stay. Instead, I reached into the tissue holder to extract a couple of Kleenex, handing one to my best friend. "I'm not sure how that went. It was supposed to be strictly punishment."

"I think we were just fooling ourselves on that one." Patrick looked disgusted as he moved away and threw himself down on the couch where we'd found Jessa a few moments before. "Did you really think we could just spank her and be done?"

"No, I guess not." I conceded the point as I sat down beside him on the other cushion and leaned my head against the headrest. "I've been wanting her for months. Hell, since before we hired her to work for us."

Patrick groaned. "Same here. I noticed her perfect little heart-shaped ass in those tight jeans she used to wear at the hot dog stand. Why do you think I started suggesting we get hot dogs every weekend?"

I grinned at him. "Why do you think I didn't remind you how unhealthy they are?"

We both groaned at the same time. "She's how old?" asked Patrick.

"Nineteen, I think. I'm pretty sure she hasn't had a birthday since she started babysitting for us."

"Nineteen. Fuck," he said in a slight roar. "She's too young."

"She's probably a virgin too." I was reasonably certain of that after having probed her tight sheath. I hadn't gone deeply enough to run into a barrier, but was fairly sure the only fingers before mine that had been inside that tight pussy might've been her own. "She might not be completely untouched, but she's definitely innocent." My dick jumped in my pants at the thought, even though a twinge of conscience pushed back the reaction. "Way, way too young and inexperienced for our kind of games."

"Yeah, I know. Girls her age want romance. They don't want just amazing sex and the contract. They want to fall in love and all that."

I sighed. "And I don't think I want *all that*." When we fell for Victoria, it had blindsided us both. I'd been just twenty-three, and Patrick was a few months younger than me.

But our eyes had met across the sex club we had just recently joined, and I swear we both loved the curvaceous Victoria at first sight—though I confessed it to Patrick before he brought it up. She was a decade older than us, and more experienced in every way, but particularly in BDSM. She liked to top and bottom, but as we gained confidence as Doms, she had become more and more submissive. We had earned her submission as we earned her love. She'd had ours too.

I smiled for a moment as I remembered the private beach ceremony we'd had in the Caribbean with the three of us standing in the surf as we exchanged rings. She had slid ours on our fingers, and we both put one on hers. That was as legal as a triad relationship like ours could get, and we'd been happy. Less than a year after that, the twins had been born, and they looked just like Patrick.

That bothered me for maybe a minute, until I held Sam, and then Tam. They weren't mine biologically, but they were mine in every other way that counted, and Patrick and I were closer than brothers anyway. He'd felt the same way when Cori came along.

"So we're agreed—hands off the nanny?" asked Patrick with a hint of hopefulness in his tone, as though he was praying I would disagree.

Remembering how painful it was to lose someone I loved as deeply as I'd loved Victoria, I nodded firmly. There was no way I was ready for that sort of emotional vulnerability again, and Jessa was too young and inexperienced to handle the two of us anyway, especially with our dominant preferences. "It's the best course of action."

With a groan, Patrick nodded and leaned back against the couch with his eyes closed. "Doing the right thing sucks."

I laughed as I leaned back and got more comfortable, though that was difficult with my still-erect cock pressing insistently against my briefs. "It sure does. Almost as much as blue balls."

Chapter Four

I'd gone straight home after that and locked myself in my bedroom. I spent the rest of the night pretending it hadn't happened and finally fell asleep around dawn. I was exhausted, but when I woke hours later, I was certain I'd dreamed about what they had done to me. My body was still humming with arousal, and I immediately put my fingers in my folds and stroked my clit until I came with a quiet moan.

After that, I got dressed as quickly as possible after a long, hot shower. I didn't want to be late for class, and it would be a busy day with three courses, so I wouldn't have time to think about what had happened last night.

At least I shouldn't have had time to think, but my classes seemed to tick by slowly, and my thoughts remained centered on what I'd allowed Patrick and Dante to do to me last night. The spanking had been weird, but not a surprising choice of discipline if they were into bondage and domination.

What had been the weirdest part was afterward, when they had both touched me in that decidedly sensual way, fingering me until I came. That was pretty far from normal employee-employer relations.

I was confused, having no idea what any of it meant. Did they expect me to be their sex toy now? Did they think I would be okay with doing whatever they wanted? Just drop my pants and flash my ass whenever either one of them wanted to spank or finger me?

I shifted restlessly in my chair as my panties grew wet again just thinking about it. Dammit, I was getting turned on by imagining being at their beck and call, flashing my ass for a spanking whenever the mood struck them. Until I tried it, I was certain I wouldn't have considered spanking sexy at all, but they had made it something far more pleasurable than I supposed a punishment was meant to be.

So if they asked me to do it again, would I?

I knew I couldn't. It was wrong, because they were my employers, and they were gay, for heaven's sake. Why would they ask *me* to do such things anyway? But they hadn't seemed gay last night. I was confused and wondered if maybe they were bisexual instead.

I was no closer to figuring out how I was going to act when it was time to pick up the twins. They were waiting for me in the pickup zone. I took their hands in each of mine, and we started walking from their exclusive preschool over to the apartment in midtown Manhattan, which was a five-block walk.

We passed the time chattering, and the walk seemed to be over far too quickly. I was letting the three of us into their apartment sooner than I had anticipated. This was part of our daily routine. I got the kids from school and dropped them off the apartment. If either one of their dads were home, my work was done, since Cori had a full-time babysitter during the day. I didn't have any responsibility for her until weekends or the occasional night. If neither one of the men were home, I stayed until one showed up.

"Dad? Papa?" called Sam.

"You home?" bellowed Tam. They both had Patrick's thick mop of brown hair and bright blue eyes, and they were identical down to the two freckles at the tip of their noses.

My heart skipped a beat when I heard Patrick call back a reply. That meant I could escape sooner, but also meant I had to face at least him, if not Dante too. Dante might or might not be home, since they seemed to split their time between the office of their computer firm and working from home.

Patrick appeared in the entryway a moment later and bent down to hug the boys. "Run into the kitchen to get your snacks. Bridget left ants on logs today."

"All right," cried Sam as he headed toward the kitchen.

Tam lingered behind for a moment. "Did she put peanut butter on mine?" He asked in such a fashion as to reveal his deep hatred for the legume.

Patrick tousle his brown hair for a moment. "Of course not. She left you cream cheese. She's a great chef, and she knows all your preferences."

"Yes." He pumped his fist in the air and went running after his brother.

I reached for the doorknob, but made the mistake of looking at Patrick uncertainly. His gaze caught me, drawing me in, and I couldn't manage to turn the knob.

"I'd like to talk to you in my office for a moment."

I sighed and nodded, knowing it was better to get it over with. I still half-expected him to fire me despite their assurance that the spanking would be my punishment. I didn't think what they had done to me last night qualified as punishment. Maybe they had reached the same conclusion, so he was going to cut me my final check and send me on my way.

Maybe he was going to apologize for what had happened. That notion was almost as hideous, simply because I didn't want to discuss it. Talking about it meant acknowledging it.

I stood awkwardly in his office, my gaze going to the bookcase that I now knew swung open to reveal an entrance to a private room. I hadn't gotten a good glimpse of what was in that room, and curiosity was burning through me again. *Curiosity killed the cat.* It hadn't killed me, but had certainly earned me a bare-bottom spanking and the first orgasm from fingers other than my own.

I cleared my throat and shifted position, still standing.

Patrick sighed, sounding annoyed. "Quit lingering in the doorway and come sit down."

I somewhat complied, moving away from the doorway to stand near the chairs, but didn't sit.

With a smothered curse, he strode around the desk and slammed the door behind me before coming up to stand beside me. He wasn't exactly encroaching in my space, but I was very aware of his presence and how close he was. It wouldn't take much to reach out and touch him. I clenched my hands to avoid the temptation to do so.

Staring straight ahead and not looking at him, I asked, "What did you need, Mr. Shelley?" He hadn't been Mr. Shelley since the second week they started coming to the hot dog stand at the park, but I felt the need to put some distance between us, even if it was symbolic.

"I wanted to apologize for scaring you yesterday. Things went farther than we planned."

Slowly, I turned my head to look at him. My tone was tart. "I expect that happens when you spank someone."

His lips twitched. "Not always, but more often than not, I suppose."

It was awkward, but I forced myself to ask the question circulating through my head. "How does that affect your relationship with Dante?"

Patrick frowned. "What'd you mean?"

"Don't you guys get jealous watching each other? And I thought you were gay, but I guess you're bi?"

He blinked before he started laughing. It was a deep belly chuckle, and he was wiping tears from his eyes a moment later. "You think me and Dante are gay?"

I arched a brow. "Yeah, it's pretty obvious. I think. You guys are practically inseparable, and you're raising the kids together. They have both your names hyphenated for their last names, and there's no mom in the picture. Did the kids have the same egg donor?"

His expression clouded. "We're raising the kids together because we're a family, and our wife, Victoria, died giving birth to Cori. There was no surrogate or donor. Just her."

I reached out to put a hand on his bicep, instinctively feeling the need to comfort him. "I'm sorry. I didn't mean to bring up sad memories with my speculation. I've just been curious for a while, but didn't want to ask."

His expression remained dark for moment, and then he blinked, and a smile appeared. "I have a feeling you're curious a lot, aren't you, Jessa?"

I blushed and shrugged. "My mom would say I'm overly inquisitive. I guess you know that after yesterday though." I looked down as my cheeks heated. I wished I'd left my long black hair down today instead of shoving it back into a ponytail so I could hide some of my embarrassment behind the thick strands.

"It's natural to be curious. For example, I'm just dying to know..." He trailed off as his fingers slipped into my hair, stroking the strands gently.

"About what?" I licked my lips as he petted the ponytail, letting locks of hair fall through his fingers.

"I'm just dying to know what your mouth tastes like."

I swallowed the sudden lump in my throat and licked my lips. "I don't know." My voice was squeaky in my nervousness.

"I think I'll just find out for myself." He spoke with confidence, but hesitated for a moment. He was clearly giving me the opportunity to pull away or say no.

I didn't have the fortitude to do so. I simply stood there and waited as he stepped closer to put his arms around me. Though his fingers had been inside me, this somehow felt far more intimate as I stared up at him and waited for his head to descend.

His lips pressed against mine in a gentle, almost teasing fashion. I had been kissed before, but had never anticipated a kiss with such eagerness previously. His lips firmed and curved to mine, and his tongue plunged inside a moment later. He grasped my ponytail to tug back my hair, which forced my neck to curve.

That gave him better access to my mouth, and he devoured me. There was no other word for it. It felt like Patrick was totally consuming me, but I was happy to lose myself in him. The kiss left me with a dripping core, aching nipples, and a pulsing need between my legs when he finally stepped back.

"Your mouth is delicious, but I bet you taste even better elsewhere."

I was pretty sure I knew what he meant, but couldn't bring myself to ask. I just bit my lip and looked down, finding it difficult to meet his gaze.

Patrick grasped my chin and forced it up gently, so that our gazes met. "Is it all right if I taste you? I want to spread you across my desk to admire that pretty little pussy before I dive in. Can I do that?"

I should've said no. That's what any sane person would do, but I was clearly nuts, because I just nodded. He extended a hand that I took and walked with him, though I still felt like I was floating through a dream. Even when he laid me across his desk and slipped off my leggings and panties after discarding my boots, I was half-convinced it was just a really vivid fantasy.

"I think we need to institute a no-pants rule. I want to be able to get to this pussy any time the whim strikes me."

My heart skipped a beat, but I didn't respond. I didn't know what to say, especially since his words seemed indicate he thought this would be an ongoing situation. I could see where he would think that, since I'd done nothing to dispel the notion. I wasn't even sure I wanted to refuse constant access to my pussy. As he bent his head, moving closer to my slick flesh, I couldn't see a reason why I would reject such tender attention anyway.

"That is an exquisite pussy. I bet it's tight, and you're clearly wet." He slid two fingers inside me slowly, as though verifying his supposition.

When he withdrew them a moment later, my body tried to grip him for a moment, and I blushed.

"You're so eager. Are you ready for me to lick that clit of yours? I want to feel your cream on my tongue and flooding my mouth."

I whimpered and shifted restlessly, turned on both by his words and his breath fanning against the most delicate part of me. It was unexplored territory, other than my own digits, and my stomach clenched with nerves as I waited for the first touch of his lips against me.

Unlike the kiss, where he had started out almost tentatively, he dove right in, as he'd said. His tongue and lips moved over me, learning my anatomy, and I started whimpering at the onslaught of sensations that threatened overwhelm me.

It was unlike anything I'd imagined, and far more intense than I had expected. It was surprising I didn't come the moment his lips pressed against my mons, let alone when his tongue squirmed into my slit to seek out my opening before moving upward to stroke firm circles around my clit.

"Dammit, Patrick! We agreed this was a bad idea." The door slammed as Dante stormed in a moment later. Even his angry expression could do nothing to stave off the orgasm that was already spiraling through me. When Patrick clamped his lips around my clit and sucked firmly, it sent me over the edge as I opened my mouth to shout my pleasure.

Chapter Five

I hurried across the room and put my hand over her mouth to keep in her cries of ecstasy. I didn't want the kids to come running to investigate. Right now, they were busy helping Cori's caretaker get ready to leave for the day, so we had a few minutes.

"We agreed," I said again.

"I know. Fuck." He groaned as he lifted his head from between her thighs, proof of her arousal gleaming on his face. "You have to taste this pussy for yourself. Then if you can walk away, you're a stronger man than me."

I shook my head, trying to remain strong, but it was difficult when I was standing so close. I could smell her arousal in the air, and her splayed legs, which she seemed unable to fully support at the moment, revealed a perfect snapshot of her sweet little pussy. Her lips were mostly closed, but there was a hint of her clit peeking out. A neatly trimmed bush matched the hair on her head, and my resolve weakened.

She moaned, looking like she was about to sit up. I had to act quickly and decide whether I was going to do the right thing or say fuck it and do what I wanted.

A trail of moisture seeped from her slit just then, and that decided it for me. I had to have a taste. I bent my head, unable to resist, and softly slid my tongue inside her. She was probably still sensitive from Patrick going down her. The man ate pussy with enthusiasm, so I tried to be gentle.

She tasted exquisite, being sweet and salty with a hint of musk that was her own personal fragrance. Her breathless moans and the way she arched her hips against my mouth were both addictive, and I couldn't move away from her. I had to catch each little drop of her cream, and I almost came in my pants when I imagined how it would be to have her come on my tongue.

Patrick was watching everything, and he was leisurely stroking his bulge, but hadn't dipped his hand inside his pants. I wasn't sure I would've had the same ability to resist if our positions were reversed, and I was watching the show rather than performing.

She was whimpering and grunting, arching her hips against me in an adorable, frantic fashion, and I increased the pace of my mouth. I started tonguing her more rapidly and darted up to circle my tongue around her clit a few times before sucking it firmly.

That must be the key to making Jessa come, because she stiffened against me, her mouth opening with a long cry that neither Patrick nor I thought to muffle, and she quaked around me. A gush of cum filled my mouth and painted my face, and I moaned my own satisfaction. I couldn't get enough of her. I wanted to keep eating that sweet little pussy all day.

I probably would've waited only long enough for her to be less sensitive before going back for seconds if there hadn't been a knock at the door a moment later. I groaned under my breath as I inhaled one last lungful of her sweet aroma and lifted my head to stand completely.

Patrick cursed as he moved away from us. He didn't open the door. "What is it?" he asked through the wood.

"We heard Jessa cry. Is she okay, Papa?" Tam's voice was full of concern.

Patrick lips quirked as I wiped my face with the back of my hand. I shared a rueful grin with him.

"She's just fine, Tam. We'll be out in a few minutes, as soon as we finish our discussion."

"Is that what you call this, a discussion?" I teased my friend as I heard our kids running down the hall.

"I do like to think I'm a cunning linguist," said Patrick with a grin.

As one, we turn to Jessa, who was just making it to her feet. She looked wrung out and overwrought. "Are you all right?" asked Patrick.

She nodded, but looked shell-shocked. "I can't believe I did that. I let you both…" She trailed off. "I probably would've fucked both of you if they hadn't interrupted." She seemed nonplussed by the idea.

My dick had a completely different reaction as I imagined sinking inside her. I knew Patrick well enough to know he'd want to be the first one inside her ass, but that meant I got her pussy. I was more than fine with that.

She suddenly looked at us, awareness returning as the haze of passion faded from her expression. "I can't ever do this again. I can't believe I did this." She seemed on the verge of hysteria for a moment.

I reached out a hand, but she jerked away. She back toward the door before turning and starting to run. I shared a look with Patrick, silently asking if he thought we should follow. When he shook his head, I knew he was right. She needed a chance to regroup and recover, but this wasn't over.

It was pretty far from over, in fact. Today had marked a turning point. She was too young and inexperienced to handle us, but she was just going to have to toughen up and get on board. We wanted her with a quiet desperation I couldn't remember feeling for a long time. I was equally certain she wanted us–both of us—with the same desperation, but she had to know exactly what we wanted from her, and she had to be willing to provide it.

I was going to be on tenterhooks as we waited to see her again to discuss our expectations and hers. If she showed up for work, that was.

Chapter Six

Jessa

I managed to avoid seeing them for no more than a few minutes in passing for the rest of the week. They were obviously trying to get me to stay and talk, but I couldn't. I just didn't know what to say to them, especially since I could barely look either one of them in the face without blushing a thousand shade of red. Just remembering what I had experienced at their hands—more their mouths than anything—was enough to embarrass and arouse me. I wanted to do it again, just as much as I didn't want to.

What was wrong with me to want two men? It was all kinds of wrong, but I couldn't seem to stop thinking about them or the possibilities. Just that morning, my mom had commented on my head being in the clouds more than usual. I had managed to laugh it off, but if she was noticing how distracted I was during the few hours she was with me between her three jobs, I must be pretty out of it.

Who could blame me though? These sorts of things didn't happen to most girls ever, and here I was with an invitation—though not yet spoken—to participate in a threesome with the two sexiest men I'd ever met.

It wasn't the threesome holding me back, though that was a little daunting. What really frightened me was what would happen after. I was too inexperienced to keep their attention for long, so it was inevitable they would dump me. I wasn't even sure we could call it dating if we ended up just fucking a few times. I was unknowledgeable about the rules and etiquette for triads. I was just certain they couldn't possibly want me for long. Once the novelty wore off, that would be it.

Would they expect me to keep working for them as though nothing had happened? I didn't think I could do that, but I also didn't want to leave my job. I loved the kids, and I loved working with them. I didn't want them to get hurt in the crossfire of our inevitable falling-out.

That was how I managed to evade them for the first few days, but they corned me on Friday, and they used my weakness to do it: The kids. I was certain they had coached them on it, because Tam sounded so stilted when he said as I started to leave Friday, "You should stay for pizza, Jessa. We can even order you a pizza with goldfish."

"It's not goldfish," said Sam as he elbowed his brother, "It's ankle bites."

I couldn't help laughing, though my thoughts were still heavy. "I think you mean anchovies, and I do love those, but I have homework."

"Please stay," said Tam, losing some of the woodenness of his words that suggested these were spontaneous rather than memorized. "We can stuff ourselves silly and eat pizza and ice cream and popcorn and watch movies. Dad and Papa said we could have anything we wanted tonight if we got you to stay."

I shot a disapproving look at both of the reprobates, but they appeared unrepentant at having been caught. "That does sound like a tempting offer." I should say no. I knew I should, but I couldn't bring myself to disappoint the two little boys who meant so much to me. Part of me also didn't want to disappoint their dads, but everything was still so ambiguous that I wasn't sure about that.

I caved. "Okay." In no time, Dante was calling for pizza while Patrick herded the children to the family room.

I slipped upstairs to the guest room, where I kept a drawer full of things, to get more comfortable for the evening. I fished out a baggy sweatshirt and leggings, and quickly stripped out of the clothes I'd worn that day for school.

By some compulsion I couldn't resist, I peeled off my plain white panties too and replaced them with a slightly sexier pair of pink satin high-cuts I kept in the drawer. They weren't exactly screaming seduction either, but they were far more attractive than the underwear I'd worn that morning. I still wasn't certain I would be showing them to anyone besides myself, but I figured it was better to be prepared.

With that in mind, I also skipped a bra. I exited to the hallway and found Dante retrieving Cori while walking out with her day-minder. I didn't know Eleanor very well, since our paths didn't cross that much, but she was a friendly older woman who flashed me a smile, and I returned it.

Cori saw me and launched herself out of Dante's arms and into mine. I'd gotten good at catching her, and I absorbed the jolt with hardly noticing. I propped her on my hip, and she laid her curly head against mine. It felt good to have her snuggle like that, though she soon started chattering. I could usually understand most of what she said, but when she was excited, she talked quickly enough that I had trouble making it out.

Fortunately, Dante and Patrick helped decipher her words throughout the evening as we ate pizza, a mountain of junk food, and watched two movies. Cori was asleep before the end of the first one, but Sam and Tam made it all the way through the end of second one and were still clamoring for a third when Dante and Patrick herded them upstairs.

"Wait for us," said Dante as he passed by me, squeezing my arm lightly.

I sighed, but nodded. I couldn't put it off forever, could I? I still wasn't sure what to do, so I'd just have to wing it and go on instinct when the time came. I busied myself cleaning up the mess while they took care of the kids, and when they returned to the family room twenty minutes later, it no longer looked like a hurricane filled with popcorn and candy had blown through.

"Thanks for cleaning up," said Patrick.

"Definitely. It's not in your job description." Dante came to stand beside me as he said the words.

I shrugged. "I figured you guys have a maid or cleaning service, but I couldn't leave a mess like that. My mom would be horrified if I did." My mother had always been a stickler for me cleaning up after myself. I'd been expected to do it from a young age, but it wasn't because she was lazy or overly strict. She was just busy working to pay the bills and put food on the table, and she didn't have time to coddle me as much as I would have liked. On the plus side, it had left me more mature than a lot of women my age.

"We want to talk to you," said Patrick.

I nodded as I sat down on the huge ottoman in front of the sofa. They took seats on the sectional facing me, and I was close enough I could have reached out and laid a hand on each of their knees if I had chosen to. I didn't though. I kept my hands to myself to avoid losing control of them and letting them wander wherever they wanted, which could be disastrous. I didn't bother with the pretense of asking about the topic of conversation. I just sat there and waited.

"I think it's obvious that we want you, Jessa." Dante spoke first.

I nodded.

"And do you want us?" asked Patrick.

I hesitated for a moment, licking my lips. "I think so, but I'm scared. There are two of you, and just one of me..." I trailed off with a shrug. "People don't do that sort of thing."

"Who cares what people do? We do what makes us happy, and we discovered early on that sharing women was better for us than having sex with them alone."

I turned to Patrick, shaking my head. "I just don't understand how you guys can be close enough to do that."

"We're like brothers," said Dante easily. He slung an arm around Patrick's shoulder in a casual fashion. "We don't share our life stories much, but you deserve a peek behind the curtain. My mom took off when I was little, and my father was a piece of crap."

I winced on his behalf. "I can relate to that. My dad disappeared before the dye finished drying on the positive pregnancy test."

"I met Patrick in middle school. I was gifted, but troubled."

"He was an asshole," said Patrick affectionately.

Dante lifted a shoulder, but didn't refute the assertion. "I hated Patrick at first. Especially when he was kind to me. I was a scholarship kid, and I wanted them all to treat me like shit. I needed them to in order to remind myself I didn't belong."

"He did a pretty good job of dissuading everyone of being his friend except me." Patrick shrugged. "I saw something special in him, and I'm a stubborn bastard."

"When we became friends, it was a tight bond, and the Shelleys were good to me too. They were kinda like surrogate parents, and when my piece of shit father finally got himself arrested for a charge that would stick—armed robbery—they offered me a place to live. They took me in and raised me as one of their own. In fact, the Shelleys adopted me when I was twenty-one. So, we are brothers in that sense."

"When did you start sharing?" I was fascinated by the story they were telling me, never having imagined that their friendship went that far back, or it had such a shaky start. I was surprised to learn Dante wasn't born with the same silver spoon in his mouth that must have been wedged firmly in Patrick's, because he handled wealth with confident assurance just like everything else.

"Jennifer Hadley," said Patrick.

Dante chuckled. "She was the one. We noticed over the years that we liked the same women. Not even the same type, but the exact same girls. It was uncanny. If one of us found a girl attractive, the other one was bound to as well. There was a little bit of rivalry here and there, but it didn't reach epic proportion until junior year of high school, when French exchange student Jennifer Hadley came to our school for a semester."

"We both wanted her badly," said Patrick. "We behaved like a couple of idiots to get her attention, and it was causing tension between us. Jennifer had an unorthodox solution. She didn't want to choose. She wanted to share, so we agreed."

"It was amazing, and a million times better than it had been alone. We just knew then."

"So you've shared women ever since then?"

"Mostly. We've occasionally had one-night stands or brief flings that were just one woman and one of us, but we always knew that we'd want someone to share long-term. When we were ready to settle down, it would be with one woman we shared."

"And that was Victoria?" I had a difficult time saying her name, almost choked by jealously, which was ridiculous. She was dead, but I could still see the love they had for her, and I didn't like it. That was irrational, but I couldn't help how I felt.

"Indeed it was. It was sooner than we expected. We had just started playing on the BDSM scene ourselves, deciding to explore it to see if we liked it. Victoria was already established, and she was an experienced dominatrix. She taught us what we needed to know and guided us to reach our full potential as Doms. More than that, she was our partner and our wife, though we couldn't legally marry her. She meant the world to us, and the three of us clicked."

"It was special," said Patrick softly.

My eyes blinked, and I felt guilty for the jealously I'd experienced a little while ago. It was obvious there had been a deep and true love between the three of them, and I was heartbroken on their behalf, even though I was still envious that Victoria had enjoyed such a bond with them. Even if I got a few nights with them, I was certain it wasn't going to lead anywhere like that. They wouldn't fall for me. I wished I could be as confident that I wouldn't fall for them, but I was afraid my heart would be broken when they tired of me and moved on.

"We've established we all want each other, but you need to know what it is we want." Dante spoke matter-of-factly.

I shifted positions slightly, leaning forward. "What is it you want?"

"We want to give you an amazing taste of our world, and we hope you'll enjoy it. Ultimately, we want to give and receive pleasure. That's what this is about."

I swallowed the lump in my throat as I searched for an answer. "I see." It was all I could manage for the moment. Dante made it sound like a short-term arrangement. Was he warning me about getting emotionally entangled?

I shouldn't go in expecting some unlikely happy-ever-after with two men. If I did this, I should regard it as a once-in-a-lifetime experience, and maybe something to cross off my sexual bucket list. I had to keep it uncomplicated and unemotional.

I didn't know if I could do that.

"There's one more thing," said Patrick. He hesitated, sharing a look with Dante that I was sure told each of them more than a ten-minute conversation could have imparted. They were that close.

"What?"

"We want to have you at the same time," said Patrick.

I frowned. "I kinda figured that, since it's a threesome."

Dante cleared his throat. "He means with us both inside you at the same time."

My butt clenched at the thought, and I was a little apprehensive. "I think we can try that—if I do this."

Patrick sighed. "Do you understand what we mean?"

I frowned at him. "I assume one of you wants to do me in the front, and the other in the back? Or would one of you be in my mouth?" I posed the question hopefully, since the idea of taking either one of them up the ass was more than a little frightening.

"We want to do that sometimes, but what he really means is we want to be inside you at the same time. Both our cocks inside your pussy simultaneously."

My mouth dropped open in shock. That wasn't even possible, was it?

Chapter Seven

As the implication of their words truly sank in, my mouth gaped open. "I don't think you can actually do that, can you?" I was squeaky as a mouse when I asked the question.

"You can, and we have. We don't expect you to be able to right away," said Patrick.

"It takes some adjustment," added Dante.

I shook my head, still disbelieving. "Why would you want to do that? You said you aren't gay." There was an accusatory tone in my voice that I didn't intend. I didn't care if they were gay or not, or if they were bisexual, but I was still shocked at what they wanted from me. It felt almost like a betrayal, the way they had sprung it on me.

"We aren't." Dante shrugged. "It's just a way to feel close as part of the triad, and it's the best way to leave it up to fate who fathers a child in this kind of relationship."

My eyes widened. "You don't mean you want me to have a baby right now?"

Patrick laughed. "No, that isn't what we want at all. We just want to make you feel good. It makes us feel good too. It's not some altruistic thing at all. It's pretty damn selfish of both of us to want to be with you considering your age and lack of experience."

Dante walked closer to me, standing just a few inches away with his arms crossed over his chest. "Which reminds me... Are you a virgin, Jessa?"

I blushed and looked away as I nodded, uncertain why I was embarrassed. I wasn't ashamed to still be a virgin. It was just awkward to discuss it with these two, especially knowing what they wanted from me. "See, it won't work."

"Not both of us at the same time to start with, but we can work up to that." Dante's hands dropped to his sides, and then he lifted one to cup my chin. "You never have to do anything with us that you don't want to, but we will push you to your limits. It's part of who we are as dominants, and I have a feeling you'll thrive as a submissive. You have the right tendencies."

I shook my head. "I really don't think I can live up to your expectations, Dante."

His fingers trailed down my face to my neck to caress the length of my carotid artery with his forefinger. "We don't have any firm expectations. Let's just see what happens."

I closed my eyes, struggling to think. I knew this was my last chance to say no and leave, but was that what I wanted? I was certain they would stop at any point if I asked them to, but instinctively guessed that would be the end of everything entirely. And I wasn't even sure I would ask them to stop, or want them to. I just felt like maybe I *should*.

"What's it going to be, Jessa?" Patrick had moved to my other side, and his voice was close now. His hand twined in my hair a moment later, stroking softly.

I opened my eyes, torn between the answer a good girl would give, and the one I wanted to say. "Things like this don't happen to girls like me."

"And girls like you don't happen to guys like us very often," said Dante in a soothing tone. "It'd be pretty stupid to pass on such an opportunity, don't you think?"

I closed my eyes again with a sigh. My surrender was inevitable and had been from the moment I entered the room, if not before. It wasn't because they had overwhelmed me or coaxed me into doing something I didn't want to do. It was far more straightforward and uncomplicated than that—I wanted them, and they wanted me. What they wanted from me was scary, and I still wasn't certain I could do it, but I wanted to try.

Opening my eyes again, I nodded at him and then Patrick. "Yes."

"In that case, let's leave this room and go to my bedroom." Dante leaned down far enough to grab my hand and take me gently from the chair as he pulled me behind him. Patrick was a few steps behind us, and I reached out for him. He closed the gap between us and took my other hand in his, and it felt righter than I'd ever imagined. We were just holding hands, but it linked me to them in a way I couldn't describe. I could only imagine how much more intense that would be after we made love.

Fucked, I forced myself to silently amend. I had to be realistic about this and accept that was all it was. This was fucking and nothing more. If tried to convince myself it was more, I would definitely get my heart broken. I couldn't do that, because I couldn't work for them if it was too painful, and I didn't want to leave the kids. I had to keep *this* separate from my other role in the household.

It was easier said than done as Dante led me into a room down the hall once we were upstairs. I knew where their rooms were, but never had any reason to go into either one. I'd thought it strange that they kept separate bedrooms when I thought they were a couple, but there were lots of reasons they might've done so. Being platonic with each other hadn't been one of the reasons I had considered though.

The room was full of dark colors and heavy furniture, so came off feeling stern and uncompromising. It was a good fit for Dante, with his forceful personality. Other than a brief glimpse at the surroundings, I paid little attention to the furniture and décor. Instead I kept my attention focused on the men in front of me.

Patrick moved behind me, and they worked in unison to undress me as quickly as possible. I barely had time to process what was happening before I was standing naked where I had been dressed less than a minute before.

I shivered, though it wasn't really cold. I was just nervous, and my nipples peaked. I crossed my arms over my chest to hide them, but froze when Dante grasped my wrists. I looked up at him uncertainly as he dragged them back to my sides.

"Don't cover your body from us. We want full access to everything."

I nodded and swallowed the lump of apprehension clogging my throat. I could do this. I *wanted* to do this, and I didn't want fear to get the best of me.

Dante took a step back and started stripping off his clothes. He'd dressed casually, so the polo and khakis were gone in seconds, soon leaving him in his boxer-briefs. From my vantage point, I couldn't see if Patrick had undressed, but he wasn't actively touching me at the moment, so I assumed he must be doing the same.

Dante hooked his fingers into the waistband of his boxer-briefs and pulled down to peel off the black cotton in one smooth motion. He placed them neatly on top of the pile of clothing on the floor before moving closer to me.

He didn't reach out for me yet, and I took advantage of the moment to admire his body in full. He had tight, toned muscles, a defined eight-pack of abs, and strong, muscular legs. I skipped over his cock for a moment before finally forcing myself to look. If I was too shy to look at it, there was no way I'd ever be able to touch it, and I wanted to. Very much.

His shaft was thick and long, jutting forward insistently as though homing in on me. The head was almost purple in his need. Pre-cum dripped from the tip of his cock, and I reached out to catch it. I didn't touch him yet, but his fluid was on my finger.

"Taste it."

Feeling uncertain, I followed Dante's suggestion—which could've been a command. I had a hard time telling the difference. The flavor of salt and slight sweetness bloomed on my tongue, along with something I couldn't identify. It was strange, but not unpleasant.

"Come here, Jessa." Dante crooked his finger at me to underscore his words.

I moved closer, aware Patrick still wasn't touching me. I look glanced uncertainly over my shoulder, concerned I'd done something that caused him to lose interest, but he appeared to be relaxed and just watching.

My gaze dropped to his cock, and his skin was a few shades lighter than Dante's golden-brown, which made his arousal all the more obvious. His shaft was full and heavy, and he was stroking it lightly. I couldn't tell if he was masturbating while watching me with Dante, or if he was simply providing himself some stimulation and support for his large shaft.

"Eyes on me, pet."

I looked back at Dante, eyes widening when I saw him point to the floor. I shrugged my confusion.

"On your knees."

I trembled with a combination of nerves and excitement as I slowly got to my knees on the floor. Dante sat down on the edge of the bed and spread his legs before indicating I should move forward. I was forced to crawl the last few steps, which was humbling, but also exciting.

When I stopped before him, he grabbed a handful of my hair, which I had left down for the evening, and used it to drag my head forward. The movement itself was aggressive, but his hold was tender, and I never felt threatened or forced as he guided my mouth the tip of his cock.

I parted my lips to take it inside, grimacing for a moment as more of his cum flooded my mouth. The sheer quantity took a moment for me to adjust to, and he hadn't even come yet. I wondered if he would expect me to swallow, and I was certain he would. I was nervous about the idea, especially since I'd never done this before.

"Are you new to this, pet?"

I looked up at him, his cock stuffed in my mouth preventing me speaking, and tried to blink a few times.

He laughed. "I'll take that as a yes. Don't be shy or tentative. Just do what you want, and if it hurts or doesn't feel good, I'll tell you."

I started out slowly, exploring the length of him as I became familiar with his flesh. He really seemed to like it when I stroked my tongue under the head of his cock, issuing moaning sounds of approval.

His hand remained firmly wrapped in my hair, and he held it like he was holding a leash attached to my head. I should've been appalled at the thought, but instead, a dark part of me thrilled at his domination. Technically, I was at his mercy, but I didn't feel like it. I felt like the one in charge as I slowly licked his cock before I started sucking and bobbing my head.

Patrick was moving around behind me, and I heard something rattle, but couldn't look away from my task to see what he was doing. He knelt down behind me a moment later, and I gasped around Dante's shaft when Patrick guided his up my slick slit, thrusting shallowly into me for a moment, before moving higher.

My gasp turned to a whimper when his head pressed against my puckered bud, and I was terrified he was going to try to enter me. He wasn't slick, except for the slight trace of arousal he'd picked up when he'd thrust lightly into me, so it was going to hurt.

He groaned and moved away. "I can't wait to be able to take that ass." He made the confession as he leaned forward to bite my shoulder before burying his face against my neck and sucking on the skin there. I shivered at the passionate onslaught, temporarily forgetting to move my mouth or tongue.

"Get on your hands and knees," said Patrick.

I looked up uncertainly at Dante, wondering if I was supposed to stop sucking his dick. He moaned and shook his head as he thrust deeper inside my mouth, the head of his cock almost bruising the back of my throat. I inferred from that action that I wasn't supposed to stop attending to him either. It took a bit of creative repositioning, but I was able to kneel with my palms on the ground but keeping my mouth wrapped around Dante.

An intriguing buzzing sound filled the air, but it was a moment before I discovered what it was. I gasped when something featherlight pressed into my slit, and then jerked almost convulsively when a small nubbin vibrated against the underside of my clit. I sobbed as a quick climax overwhelmed me.

"I think our little pet isn't used to toys, Patrick."

"I guess not, Dante. Let me turn down the intensity. We don't you to come again so quickly, Jessa."

A moment later, the buzzing inside me eased to a far lower frequency. It was enough to keep me on the edge of climax without pushing me over.

"Let me just secure this so it doesn't fall out." As Patrick spoke, his fingers moved over my hips and back. Soft Velcro straps pressed against my skin a moment later.

"That's a pretty sight," said Patrick with a low whistle. "It opens up your pink pussy nicely, and you're so wet. Juices are just trickling down her thighs, Dante. It makes me want to taste. But then there's her tempting ass, which is gaping open to show her your charms. Where do I start?"

I trembled when his head pressed against my skin, his hair tickling my buttocks before his tongue dipped into my opening. It seemed like he was scooping out the cream he found there and savoring every drop. I was enjoying it too, but wasn't convinced the toy wedged in my pussy was a good thing. It was enough stimulation to make me crazy, but not enough to let me come. I suspected that was what they wanted, and I was trying to go with it, but wished they would either remove it or turn it up.

I finally remembered to start sucking Dante again, and he'd been patient. Now, he stroked the back of my head after releasing the tight hold he'd had on my hair, and his hips started to buck upward. He was feeling larger and tighter in my mouth, and I was certain he was pretty close to coming. Part of me wanted to break away before that happened, but another part wanted to know what it was like to have him fill my mouth with his cum.

When Patrick's tongue moved upward, I cried out in shock as it circled my hole. His hands cupped my buttocks, and he spread my cheeks apart, so he'd have better access. When his tongue slipped inside me, I tried to squirm away. I was so shocked by what he was doing that I couldn't enjoy it for a moment.

"Just relax, pet." Dante stroked a finger down my cheek. "Patrick is practically obsessed with asses. He would've made a great gay man."

Patrick said something, but his words weren't audible with his mouth pressed against my ass. Whatever it was he said didn't sound flattering.

"I'm going to come now, and I want you to take it all and swallow like a good pet." As he spoke, Dante cupped my cheeks in his hands, keeping my head immobile so I couldn't move away. "Are you ready?"

I nodded the best I could with him holding my face, though I wasn't sure I was actually ready. I found out less than a second later as he started to twitch inside my mouth while spurts of cum slammed into the back of my throat and painted the roof of my mouth.

It was a lot more than I'd expected, and I almost choked. It seemed impossible to be able to swallow it all, but when I looked up at him with the intention of pleading for him to let me go, and saw the care in his eyes, I couldn't bring myself to ask. I wanted to please him, so I forced myself to keep swallowing.

When he finally pulled away a moment later, I swallowed the last drops remaining on my tongue and wanted to preen for having completed the task to his satisfaction. His hands relaxed around my face, and he stroked his fingers through my hair before releasing me.

Before I had a chance to orient myself, Patrick was shifting me forward so that my face was almost against the carpet. I rested my cheek on my folded arms as I realigned myself, automatically adjusting to his unspoken commands.

The tip of something slid into my ass, and I stiffened until warm liquid filled me, along with the sound of a bottle dispensing fluid. Judging from the thick and slippery substance inside me, it had to be lube.

Patrick pressed a finger inside me, going slowly to start with, but soon sliding in another one as my body yielded to his mastery. With the toy buzzing in my pussy, and the extra stimulation in my ass, I was approaching an orgasm.

As though he sensed that, he withdrew his fingers. I groaned with annoyance before whimpering, practically begging him to keep doing what he'd been doing.

Apparently, Patrick put the *sadistic* in BDSM, because he didn't return to my neglected ass for a moment. When he did, it wasn't his fingers pressing there. Instead, was something cool and smooth, and I tentatively identified it as metal. "What are you doing to me?"

"Stretching you out. You can't take a cock in your ass easily without preparation."

I nodded and tried to relax as the strange object invaded me. At first, it was simply uncomfortable, especially when he wedged it deeper inside me. When I took a few deep breaths and forced myself to relax, the pain faded. It wasn't doing anything to excite me, but at least it didn't hurt.

"I think she's ready for you, Dante."

I looked up to peer over my shoulder at Patrick. "Ready for what?"

"Are you ready for me to be inside your pussy? Patrick wants first shot at your ass, so that means I get your pussy first. If you're agreeable, that is?"

I shrugged. "I guess so." I'd known when I entered the room that I would be leaving not a virgin, but was still afraid now that the moment was at hand.

"But he's wrong. You aren't ready just yet." Dante patted the bed beside him. "Come up here and lie down on your back."

It was awkward getting to my feet with the toy between my legs, and the metal cylinder in my ass. Patrick helped me to my feet, and I shuffled with small steps over to the bed. When I sat down, I was convinced the butt plug would pop out, but it remained inside me. Even when I scooched back so I could lie more comfortably on the bed, it didn't go anywhere.

I let out a shaky breath when the new position shifted the toy inside me enough to make it suddenly feel very good. It was no longer something to tolerate, but to savor. I pressed my ass against the bed and circled my hips, needing something more to feel complete.

"That's a fucking beautiful sight," said Dante, his voice thick with approval.

A moment later, he turned from sitting beside to lying across me, and his mouth was against mine. He kissed me firmly and thoroughly, leaving my head spinning and my lungs starved for oxygen when he finally lifted his head a moment later.

"I love your mouth." He dipped his thumb in the corner, between my lips, as he said the words.

I responded by nipping him lightly before I started to suck on the digit.

He moaned. "You have an amazingly talented mouth, and if you've never given a blowjob before, it's a safe bet that you're a natural."

I couldn't reply with his thumb in my mouth, but I smiled at him as best I could, pleased by the compliment.

"But as much as I love your mouth, there's one part of you that tastes even better." He withdrew his thumb from my mouth, tugging it free when I didn't immediately release him. His tongue slid on my body a moment later, pausing to taste each of my nipples before imparting a playful nip on the right nipple. After that, he veered strictly south, taking no further detours until he arrived at his destination seconds later.

He was inside me, carefully parting my folds with his thumbs to hold me open. His tongue glided over me like molten silk, and I whimpered as I pressed against him. The toy was still inside my pussy, preventing him from getting close enough to my clit to actually suck on it, but he licked around the edges, which made me buck my hips. I had a brief thought that maybe I shouldn't do that, in case it dislodged the toy in my backside, but I was soon too far gone to care if it did.

Dante moved his tongue lower, pausing to nibble down my lips before reaching my opening. He splayed me even farther apart with his fingers, and I could visualize what he was seeing—a sopping wet pussy eager for something to fill it.

His tongue slid inside me, thrusting rapidly and lapping up my juices as quickly as I created them. I clutched the covers and almost screamed as I started to come, finding it so much more intense with the toy on my clit, butt plug in my ass, and his face buried inside my slit.

Patrick moved quickly, clapping his hand over my mouth. "You're going to have to learn to be quieter, pet." He had picked up Dante's endearment for me, which bothered me. I wondered how many other women had become nothing but "pet" in their bedroom, which threatened to derail me from the pleasure coursing through me. My orgasm came then, and I lost the ability to worry about anything for a moment as the world dissolved around me before returning with sharper focus.

"We need something in that mouth to keep you occupied." As he spoke the words, Patrick grasped his shaft in one hand and moved the hand off my mouth to slide under my head. He cupped the back of my head as he pressed the tip of his cock between my lips. I parted willingly for him, wanting to take him inside me wherever I could.

Once Patrick was fully in my mouth, going as far into my throat as he could, Dante grasped my thighs and lifted me into the air, spreading my legs so the tip of his cock could nestle against my opening. Even in my current state of blissed-out pleasure, I was aware it wasn't his bare skin touching me. He'd slipped on a condom while Patrick was taking possession of my mouth.

"This is going to hurt, but I think it's better to get it over with. After the pain fades, I'll make sure you feel really good, Jessa."

I liked my name on his lips, preferring it to "pet" from either one of them. It wasn't anonymous, and it couldn't apply to just any woman. Jessa was all mine, and it told me that they knew it was me there with them, not just a random chick.

"I've never done this before," said Dante, sounding strained.

I widened my eyes and arched a brow, skeptical about that claim. Cori proved otherwise.

"He means he's never fucked a virgin before," said Patrick. His face was stained red with exertion, and he was pumping his hips as I sucked with enthusiasm despite twinges from my jaw. It wasn't used to such an oral workout.

With a shuddering sigh of his own, Dante slid inside me in one quick thrust. I grimaced and grunted at the pain, which radiated outward in waves for a moment. For a brief second, I was sure I couldn't endure it and thought about pulling away. Before the thought had even fully formed, the pain was already easing.

He just stayed inside me for a moment, probably giving my body a chance to adjust. I was thankful for him doing so, because I felt overly stuffed. Perhaps it was because there was a plug in my ass, or maybe I would've felt this overly filled sensation anyway, since he was so large, and I was still so tight. Either way, it took my body a moment to relax and start to enjoy what he was doing.

His first few thrusts were painful, but each one hurt less than the last, and soon enough, I was feeling only pleasure.

"Let's get rid of this," said Patrick. He sounded like he was gritting his teeth as he spoke.

A moment later, his hand went between my legs, and then the toy was gone. I looked up hopefully, thinking he might pull out the plug too, but he was clearly done. He returned his hand to my breast to start playing idly with my nipple, alternating between tugging gently and sharply. The little pulses of pain embarrassed me, because they only made me more excited and brought me closer to coming.

"She so fucking tight. I'm afraid to move and hurt her."

"You won't hurt her deliberately, Dante. Just relax and do what comes naturally. Same goes for you, Jessa."

I nodded as best I could with his shaft in my mouth.

Dante didn't verbally respond, and I couldn't see him well enough from my current vantage point to see if he nodded or shook his head. He must've agreed with Patrick's words, because he started the thrust again, moving deeper this time, and faster as well.

My body seemed to know what to do and thrust against him to meet each inch of cock he offered me. We moved in sync, and I could feel an orgasm building up inside me.

"You about ready to come?"

I opened my eyes, suddenly realizing I'd closed them in my ecstasy. I tried to relay my readiness to Patrick, and he must have understood what I was trying to tell him with my eyes.

"I'm ready too," said Dante, his breathing raspy.

"It won't take much for me to get there either. Suck hard on the head of my cock, Jessaa." Patrick gave the instructions as he thrust deeply into my throat before pulling back several inches to allow me to focus the majority of pressure on his head.

An orgasm broke over me, wiping out awareness of anything for a moment, though I was certain Dante stiffened before his cock twitched inside me. Patrick came, his seed sliding down my throat easily in my current position. It seemed fitting that we had come together, and I was an exhausted, sated lump of goo afterward.

Patrick disappeared as Dante lifted me into his arms to carry me into the bathroom. Patrick stood there, and he had started a bath. The tub was clearly big enough for the three of us, and Dante stepped right in, still holding me on his lap. Patrick joined us a moment later, and I laid my head on his shoulder. I basked in the moment, unable to do anything else besides cuddle with them after that exhausting, but amazing, lovemaking. At the moment, I couldn't bring myself to think of it as fucking.

Chapter Eight

Dante

The week seemed to pass with glacial slowness. There were no further opportunities until Friday to taste Jessa's charms again. Our workload was heavy, she had college classes, and the children seemed to always be underfoot. I loved them, but it was a relief to put them to bed Friday night.

Jessa was waiting for us downstairs, just like she'd been last Friday. She had seemed a little reluctant to stay when the boys suggested pizza and movies again, and I was anticipating we would have to allay some of her fears. She'd had a whole week to process what had happened, and she'd either worked herself into a state, or perhaps she'd accepted what was happening. That seemed unlikely, since she sat between the boys and seemed to be keeping a distance between herself and us.

Cori was sleep finally, and we tiptoed out of her room to avoid waking her. The twins had crashed a half-hour before, falling asleep partway through the second Disney movie.

"I've been looking forward to this all week," said Patrick. "I wonder if she paid any attention to my email."

When it had been difficult to find a moment alone with Jessa throughout the week, Patrick had grown desperate and ordered her a set of plugs that he overnighted to her address and emailed instructions for how to use them. He wanted her to be prepped and ready to take him up the ass this weekend, so I knew he would be highly disappointed if she hadn't done as he'd instructed. He'd probably paddle her ass—though he preferred his flogger.

We went down together, finding her still sitting on the couch. I was afraid she might've rushed out when she had the chance, since she looked apprehensive. The way she was hugging herself radiated "keep away" when all I wanted to do was get closer. I sighed.

"You're getting worked up over nothing," said Patrick. He must've read her signals too.

She blinked and looked at him. "What are you talking about?"

"It's obvious you worked yourself into a state over what happened last weekend. Let me guess, you decided you were a filthy slut, and we shouldn't do naughty things. That's the reason nobody talks about those kinds of things or admits to doing them, right?" I was bored as I listed several of the reasons I'd heard over the years for why it was wrong to have a triad, or to be in a polyamorous relationship, or to have multiple husbands or wives. I was blasé, but she was going through the anxiety of it all for the first time.

Her lower lip wobbled for a moment, and then firmed. Her eyes snapped with anger, and she got to her feet. She marched closer to me. "You don't have to be such a jerk and make fun of me."

"I wasn't." I softened my voice and put a hand on her shoulder as Patrick cupped her other shoulder with his hand. "It's just we've heard all this, and this kind of anxiety isn't uncommon, especially when you first start exploring the lifestyle. You're going to talk yourself out of this thing with us because you feel like you should. If it genuinely feels wrong, or you didn't enjoy it, then that's different. But if you're just having anxiety because you're worried what other people might think, or feel like your sex life is abnormal, don't. We're asking you not to throw away what's happening here."

She let out a frustrated sigh. "It's just so weird. People don't do these things."

"They do, but they don't necessarily talk about it. We're not asking you to broadcast our sex lives to the world. If you want to be discreet, we can do discreet. Just don't feel guilty for having both of us."

She sighed, and some of her tension seemed to melt away. "I keep telling myself that, but then those moments of panic overwhelm me. What if my mom finds out? What if she disowns me?"

Patrick put an arm around her waist and side-hugged her. "You're fretting for nothing. We're not going to tell anyone if that's what you want, and unless you confess to your mom, it won't come up."

She nodded, and though her lips were still a bit wobbly, they were far less shaky than they had been. In general, she seemed more in control. "Yeah, you're right. I shouldn't feel guilty or embarrassed for enjoying what happened last weekend. Or wanting to do it again," she whispered as her head bent, hair obscuring her features.

I chuckled as I pushed back the long strands, finding her face was as red as I'd expected. "We want the exact same thing, Jessa."

She licked her lips and looked up at me, seeming a little shy. "I like it when you call me Jessa. I don't like 'pet.'"

I frowned. "Why not?"

"It's so impersonal. I could be any woman. You could just use the endearment instead of taking the time to learn someone's name. Does that make sense?" Her blue eyes were huge in her face, revealing her anxiety at asking the question.

"It makes total sense." I leaned forward to press a kiss to her forehead, though I wanted to get far more carnal than the chaste touch.

"Did you get my email and present?" asked Patrick with a hint of eagerness. He'd apparently decided it was safe to broach the topic now that she had admitted she wanted to do it all again.

"I did." Her face when even redder. "And did what you said."

His eyes gleamed with interest, and his hand moved from her waist to the waistband of her jeans. I chuckled as his fingers dipped inside, and then he whistled a moment later. "Good girl. That has to be the biggest one."

She stuttered a bit. "I...I was...mot...motivated to get to the biggest size as soon as possible. I figured you'd want to..." She waved her hand as she trailed off. "This weekend."

"And you want to?" asked Patrick.

She nodded, though she didn't quite look at either one of us. "Very much. I'm surprised how much I like the plugs."

"Let's move elsewhere." I took one of her hands, and Patrick took the other. By unspoken agreement, we detoured from the direction that would take us upstairs to one of our bedrooms to walk down the hall toward our office—and the secret room behind the wall.

She stumbled for a moment and stopped walking. "Where're we going?"

"Our dungeon."

She shivered against me. "Do you have to call it that, Dante?"

Patrick laughed. "That's just the general term everyone uses. We're not planning to keep you prisoner or torture you. We just want to show you a few things to see what you like and don't like as we play."

After a moment, she started walking again, looking more confident. That lasted until we stepped through the secret entrance, with her mumbling something about *Scooby Doo*, and then into the dungeon.

It wasn't like a lot of BDSM dungeons. We preferred a more sterile look, with clean white walls and floors, lots of lighting, and all of our toys and gadgets arranged on shelves and racks around the room. That still left plenty of room for a St. Andrew's cross, a spanking bench, and a sex swing.

She was clearly apprehensive as she looked around, but she didn't run out of the room. "I'm not sure about all this."

"Just try to relax and see what you think. Keep an open mind." As Patrick give the advice, he started unbuttoning her blouse.

I moved behind her and reached around to unsnap and unzip her jeans before pushing them down. I was amused to see she wore sexy black underwear that was quite a bit more seductive than the pretty silky panties she'd worn last week. She'd been unsure of continuing, but she wanted to badly enough that she had prepared for it. I was encouraged by signs of her persistence. We had her naked in seconds, working together with familiarity.

Patrick claimed the honor of removing the plug she'd left in her ass at his instruction. I wondered if she'd worn it all day, or if she had "cheated" and put it in before picking up the boys and bringing them home. For the sake of her tender ass, I hoped she had spent a lot of time playing with the plugs this past week, because Patrick's large shaft would be a challenge for any woman, but especially an anal virgin.

As Patrick started undressing, I reached into a nearby cupboard and removed a corset. It was just a training one and felt slightly constrictive without actually constraining her. Plus, it would make her boobs perkier, which was always a welcome sight.

She stiffened for moment when I slid the leather around her front, but didn't tell me no. She stood passively as I finished hooking it on her, choosing the loosest setting.

"How does that feel?"

She frowned as she turned to look at me. "It's a little tight, but I guess it's okay."

I couldn't take my gaze off her breasts, which were suddenly pointing upward and straining outward, as though eager for my lips. "It makes your already-sexy body look even more tempting, which should be impossible."

I dipped my head to suck firmly on her left nipple, and she started to moan. I couldn't resist reaching between her thighs to probe her pussy, finding her slick with need. The way she pressed close to me suggested she was eager as hell. I was experiencing the same thing, hovering on the edge of coming, so I had to pull back and take a moment to cool down before I rushed her through the experience.

When Patrick was back to give her attention, I took a step away to shed my clothes, which I hung in the small closet space that was part of the cabinet. I reached for my paddle and handed Patrick his preferred flogger. Her eyes are wide when she saw the implements, but she didn't tell us to stop.

"You seemed to like spanking, so we thought we'd start with that, but with a little more intensity. Kneel down on the spanking bench."

She looked around the room, gaze settling on the correct device. "That thing?" At my nod, she walked over to it with a sigh. It took her a moment to figure out how to position herself, but when she did, my naked cock twitched at the sight. It was beautiful to see her spread and splayed like that with her rounded ass cheeks just waiting to be marked and turned red. I backed up though, allowing Patrick to go first. The flogger was an easier experience, and I wanted her to enjoy what we did, not dread it, or put up with it to please us.

She was clearly nervous, and the muscles in her ass were tight as Patrick trailed the flogger down her crack, feathering leather tendrils across her skin. He continued to caress her that way until she visibly relaxed. When she'd done so, he brought back the flogger and slapped her lightly on the back with it.

She jumped, but it had to be from surprise rather than pain, because that light touch wouldn't have hurt anyone. Patrick repeated it again, alternating between her back and her ass cheeks with light strokes. Gradually increasing the intensity, he started focusing solely on her ass. The back was a dangerous place for whipping if you didn't know anatomy well. I knew Patrick did, but he was clearly trying to avoid frightening her during her first flogging.

This was a new experience for us too. When we had really gotten into the scene, Victoria had been our guide. Since her death, we'd shared a few subs and had participated in various scenes at the private club we all took turns hosting meetings for, but every woman we'd been with had known what to expect. They were into this like we were. They weren't virgins to the lifestyle. They sure as fuck hadn't been virgins in any capacity, unlike sweet Jessa. Though no longer a virgin, she was practically still as inexperienced as one.

After a few more swats, Patrick stepped back and gestured me forward. My cock jumped with anticipation as my stomach clenched with a hint of nerves. I didn't want to scare or hurt her, but I couldn't wait to crack my paddle across her sweet ass.

With enough force, the bamboo paddle could strike firmly enough to leave a red imprint that would last for hours, but I forced myself to be gentle. I barely tapped her the first few times. It wasn't until she was squirming and writhing, arching her back and lifting her ass in the air for more, that I allowed a hint of force with the next spank.

She cried out, clearly surprised and probably in a little pain, but she didn't stop. She simply nodded, and I did it again.

I forced myself to stop after three more smacks, not wanting to bruise her. There were times when I occasionally liked to leave those kind of marks, but it usually happened during an intense scene, when both the sub and I were very into it.

Jessa wasn't in subspace, which was the only time I would consider hitting hard enough to leave marks that didn't fade after a little while. When it came to subspace, she might not ever get there, and that was okay. I was just glad she was willing to try something like this with us. If all she ever wanted was light BDSM play, we'd be happy to give her just that.

Patrick had returned his flogger to the rack while I paddled her, and now he lifted her to her feet. He took a seat on the bench and spread her across his lap, and I handed him a bottle of oil that he squirted liberally across her ass and his hand before he started soothing the reddened skin.

"Oh, I like this." She practically purred like a kitten as he continued to rub her cheeks gently.

"So do I." Patrick continued rubbing her with one hand while his other was occupied with parting her crevice to look at her asshole. Some of the oil had leaked between her cheeks, and she was gleaming there. His finger slipped inside her easily and was soon joined by a second and third.

"She's definitely been stretching." He sounded ecstatic.

I grinned, happy for him. There would be times I'd want to fuck her in the ass too, but it wasn't quite the fetish for me that it was for Patrick. I was more inclined to eat her pussy for hours than play with her ass.

I stopped short for a moment when I realized I was thinking about this in a long-term way, already imagining the other things we could show her and do to her. I shook my head to dispel the thought. This was just fucking while indulging the attraction between us. This wasn't about establishing a future with her.

I walked over to a shelf and removed a set of nipple clamps while Patrick continued to finger her ass. When I returned to them, I dropped on the floor on my knees, so I could better reach her breasts. I reached for one and fastened the clamp. "This will be a little uncomfortable, but when the sensation returns, you're going to go crazy with how good it feels."

She looked uncertain, but she was clearly submitting, and she didn't seem to have to force herself to do so. There was genuine curiosity and desire in her, and I was even more firmly convinced that Jessa was a natural submissive. She just needed some guidance to establish her preferences and learn some discipline.

A moment later, Patrick stood up with her in his arms. He skipped the sex swing in favor of the St. Andrew's cross. He bound her in the classic spanking position, with her stomach against the cross, though I was certain he was done spanking her. He just couldn't wait any longer to claim her ass as his, and that was the best position to do it.

I handed him the bottle of oil, and he got her slick before sliding on the condom and liberally coating it with the anal lube I handled him next. She stiffened when he brought the head to her anus, but didn't try to pull away. She grimaced when he gained the first couple of inches, but relaxed as he took her with gentle persistence. Watching him slowly sink inside her was sexy as hell, and I had a new understanding of his ass appreciation upon seeing how hers curved lovingly around him.

"How are you doing, Jessa?" I asked the question after I walked around to the other side of the cross and looked at her through the V there. "Does it feel okay?"

She was breathing hard, but she nodded. "Amazing."

It looked amazing, and I wanted to be part of the moment. I started undoing the bonds around her wrists and ankles. Patrick clearly guessed what I wanted, because he lifted her off the cross and laid down on a nearby vinyl mat with her atop him, never slipping out of her ass.

I stopped long enough to grab a condom from the box on the shelf and sheath myself before kneeling down between her legs. She was clearly nervous, so I put a hand on her face to cup her cheek. "Tell us if this hurts too much. It should be similar to what we did last week with a cock and fingers, but if it's too much, we can stop or slow down."

"I know you'll take care of me." The simple words were heartfelt and obviously sincere.

For some reason, they hit me like someone had driven a hammer into my solar plexus, and I had a difficult time drawing in a deep breath for a moment. The open vulnerability and trust shining in her gaze was unexpected. I wasn't sure how to react or how to feel. We had sworn off anything long-term for a long time into the future.

For one thing, we didn't want to bring subs in and out of the kids' lives, and long-term BDSM relationships usually involved living together to be a fully satisfying arrangement. For another, loving and losing Victoria had been the best and worst moments of our lives, and neither of us was ready for that kind of commitment again. Were we?

I wasn't so sure about that as I slowly guided my cock into her pussy, moving in the tiniest increments I could manage to give her body time to adjust to both of us. The way she was so open to me, both emotionally and physically, put a lump in my throat.

I coughed to clear it as I finally sank fully inside her and started moving in tandem with Patrick. We had done this often enough to have a natural rhythm, and she seemed to enjoy it. Her breathless moans and little whimpers of pleasure gave her away.

I waited until I could feel her starting to come, her sheath contracting around me, before I removed the nipple clamps. She screamed for a moment before clapping her hand over her mouth. I grinned at her. "It's soundproof in here, so you can make all the noise you want."

She didn't continue screaming, but her hand fell away from her mouth as she grunted and started waving her hands in front of her nipples. "What did you do to me?"

"Just wait." I bent my head to lick one, almost surprised that she let me.

After a moment, the pleasure must have overcome the brief pain, leaving her moaning and writhing. Reluctantly, I lifted my head so I could drive deeply inside her pussy while Patrick thrust inside her ass for the last time.

She came first, and then Patrick, and finally me. As I gave in to the pleasure slipping over me, I was alarmed by how close I felt to her, and how much I wanted to keep her with us. It was a frightening thought, but when I imagined sending her away, that was even worse. Opening myself up to the possibility of losing that kind of love again terrified me, but it wasn't half as horrifying as contemplating letting her walk away without finding out how and where these emotions could lead us.

Chapter Nine

Patrick

We finally took her to bed sometime around dawn, having exhausted her with our continued demands and innovative ways of fucking her. There was still one thing left to do, but she hadn't yet indicated she was ready for that. I couldn't blame her, but I was impatient. I'd her ass and her pussy throughout the night, but I wanted all of her. And I wanted to share it with my best friend.

She was asleep in my bed, and I had been just a moment before, until the alarm woke me. Dante stirred on her other side, and we both groaned. The kids would be up in a little while, so we needed to get her back to the guest room before then, but we hadn't been able to stomach the idea of sleeping without her between us, even if it was just for a couple of hours.

"She's so gorgeous." Dante sounded infatuated as he ran his fingers down her side. She didn't stir.

"And exhausted," I said with a satisfied chuckle. We'd clearly worn her out.

"I've been doing some thinking." Dante looked up, and his expression was serious.

"Should I be afraid?"

He shook his head. "I don't think so. I'm not ready for this to be over. I don't want her to go anywhere. How about you?"

I frowned for a moment, focusing on logistics. "We decided not to have a full-time sub until after the kids were much older."

He shrugged a shoulder. "True, but they adore her, and I doubt they'd mind having Jessa living with us."

I was sure they wouldn't, but I wasn't convinced it was a good idea. "What happens if she leaves us? The kids will be very bonded to her by then."

"She's less likely to leave us if we offer her some kind of permanence and a sign that we want more from her than just a few nights of fucking."

Dante had a point, and I nodded. "It's not that I don't want to keep her. I do, and I...care more than I expected." *Care* was a tepid word, but I wasn't sure I was ready to use anything more serious or committed just yet.

"I...care about her too." He grabbed a handful of hair and let it fall through his fingers as he stared at her whimsically. "She's just about perfect."

He sounded like a lovestruck teenager, and I recognized the expression and the tone of voice. I'd first seen it, to a lesser extent, in high school. Before discovering the joys of sharing, he'd fallen hard for a girl I had liked, but hadn't liked as much as he did. I stepped back and watched, helplessly, as she broke his heart.

The next time I'd seen that look and heard him speak that way was just after we'd met Victoria. In fact, it was after our first night together. Dante told me then that he was going to fall in love with her, and he was confident I'd do the same. I'd laughed it off, but damned if the bastard wasn't right. I'd fallen head-over-heels for Victoria too, and it had felt right between the three of us.

So did this. I didn't want her to go either. "Should we offer her a contract then?"

"Yes."

She started to stir then, and Dante helped her sit up. She looked like a woman who'd been fucked all night and slept only a couple of hours, but she was still utterly adorable and sexy as hell with her tousled hair and sleepy expression.

"What contract?" she asked, almost mumbling.

We shared a look, not realizing she'd been awake enough to hear our conversation.

"How much did you hear?" asked Dante.

"Just something about offering a contract. For me?" She blinked owlishly.

I forced my gaze away from observing her adorable morning expressions to focus on the topic. "We were just talking about how much we'd like to keep you."

She frowned. "Keep me? For how long?"

Dante answered when I let the silence stretch. "For however long we all want that. The contract just ensures that you're provided for, and that you're willing to be our sub. Depending on how elaborate we go, it can spell out all the details of what you will and won't do—and our responsibilities too—in minutiae, but I'm not inclined to put those in place. I'd rather just explore and play like we have been and find out what you like and don't like."

The sleepiness was clearing from her eyes, and her expression was difficult to read. "You want to contract me as your submissive?" Her tone and shifting facial movements revealed she was clearly appalled at the idea. "No way in hell."

I shared a puzzled look with Dante. "It's actually pretty standard in a relationship like this, Jessa. It protects you even more than it does us."

She made a huffing sound as she rolled from my bed and strode to the door. She was as naked as she'd been when I put her there a couple of hours ago.

"Jessa, come back here so we can discuss this." Dante used his firmest Dom voice, and it should've worked.

Instead, she gave him an obscene gesture over her shoulder and continued marching. My door slammed a moment later, and we stared at each other in surprise. It hadn't gone well at all, and I still wasn't certain what we'd done wrong.

Chapter Ten

Jessa

The nerve of them. I was still fulminating about it on the subway ride back to my apartment. At that point, I wasn't sure I'd ever venture back to their apartment again. I'd packed everything I kept in the guest room and stormed out. They'd tried to stop me, both asking me to stay and talk, but I wasn't in the mood for that. What I was contemplating was too violent for me to be fit company at the moment. I was simply enraged by what they had done.

The worst part was, I didn't think they even understood why I was upset. That simply underscored for me the differences in our perspectives, while showing me I had been kidding myself. I couldn't have just a physical relationship with them. I'd gotten too far in too fast, and my heart was shattering.

Being offered a contract as their submissive was an insult compared to what I wanted from them. I didn't want a contract that spelled out the terms of our relationship and provided a contingency for everything. I wanted a real relationship, with the messy blurring of rules, the daily struggles, and the occasional moments of anger, along with spontaneous bliss. They wanted me to be their sub, and I wanted to be far more.

When I reached my apartment, I groaned when I saw Mom sitting at the table. "Shouldn't you be working the morning shift at the diner?"

She glanced at the clock. "I need to be there in about forty minutes. You're home very late." Her tone was neutral.

"Or very early, depending on your perspective. I told you I was babysitting for Dante and Patrick."

My mom arched a dark brow at me. It was like looking in a slightly older, more skeptical mirror, since we looked so much alike. "Please don't insult my intelligence. I'm sure you were there with the children for part of the time, but there's clearly something more going on. You're obviously involved with one of them, which is fine. You're an adult and free to make your own decisions—but an adult wouldn't feel the need to lie about it."

I shrugged, realizing she was correct. "I didn't know you'd guessed, but I'm not really ready to discuss it."

Mom nodded. "Fair enough. Can you at least tell me which one it is?"

I started to refuse, but hesitated. Her words about an adult not lying or hiding it struck me anew. "Actually, it's both of them."

Mom dropped her cup of coffee into her saucer hard enough to make coffee splash on the table and send a chip of porcelain flying off. "What?"

With a sigh, I went to the paper towels to rip off a couple before moving to the table to clean up the mess. "It's both of them. You know how I thought they were gay?"

She nodded. "You seemed fairly certain, but not certain enough not to have a crush on them."

I blushed. "Either you've tapped into your mom superpowers, or I was just that terrible at hiding my feelings. Anyway, they aren't gay. The children had the same mother, who was also their wife. They shared Victoria."

Mom still looked shocked, but she didn't immediately launch into a tirade against them. She appeared to be choosing her words carefully. "Are they still in love with Victoria?"

The question surprised me, because I expected Mom to be far more judgmental and focus on the fact that I was involved with two men, not worry about me getting involved with men who still loved their deceased wife. "I'm sure they'll always love her, but I don't think they're still in love with her to the point where they can't move on." I felt that in my heart, but I wasn't so confident in my brain after they had offered me the second-class deal of submissive-by-contract.

"Do you think they can make you happy?"

I shrugged. "I think so, but I'm not sure if there's any future in it."

"It's probably for the best if there isn't a future, but if you decide to try to make things work, you have my support."

I blinked, mouth hanging agape. "Are you sure? I mean, it's two guys at the same time."

Mom grimaced and lifted her hand. "For the love of god, spare me the details. I love you no matter what you decide to do, and I'll support your choices. I won't pretend like it will be easy for me, and there will be some adjustment, but I'm your mother. It's my job and privilege to be here when you need me."

Tears came to my eyes then, and I started sniffling as a bent down to hug her. "Thanks, Mom." Tears continued to seep from my eyes, and I wasn't crying just because her words touched me. Emotional fallout from the last few hours, combined with stress and even the ecstasy over the last week couple of weeks, finally got to me.

At that moment, the doorbell rang. My stomach clenched with dread, and I was certain I knew who would be on the other side even as I walked toward it on laden feet that seemed impossible to move more than an inch or two at a time.

The doorbell rang again, but I was still going slowly. "You gonna answer that, or not?" asked Mom, sounding impatient.

With a sigh, I forced my feet to move faster and reached the door far sooner than I was ready to. I left the chain on, but didn't bother to peek through the peephole. It was no surprise to see Dante and Patrick standing on my doorstep. It was only surprising it had taken them this long, but I guessed they had to wait for a sitter to arrive before following me.

I frowned at them. "What do you want?"

"We want to find out why you stalked off like that. Open the damn door."

I flinched when Dante bellowed the words.

Mom's chair scraped across the floor as she got up, and she marched across the room. I wanted to stop her when she flung off the chain and opened the door with a flourish. She was short like me, but seemed unintimidated by Dante looming over her. "If that's the way you talk to my daughter, no wonder she came home crying this morning."

I swiped at my cheeks, which were still damp. "That's not true. I wasn't crying when I got home." I had just been on the verge of it.

Dante opened his mouth, and then he seemed to deflate. "I'm sorry. It wasn't my intention to shout at her or hurt her feelings. I'm just frustrated. She left without any explanation as to why."

I crossed my arms over my chest and glared at him. "That's a lie. You know exactly why I left."

"We don't," said Patrick with earnestness that was hard to disbelieve. "Will you please talk to us?"

My mother opened the door wider. "Come in and settle this. I'm on my way to work, so I'll give you some privacy."

"Thank you, Mom." My throat was thick for a moment as gratitude overwhelmed me at my mom's awesome attitude. It wasn't completely unexpected, because she was open-minded in her daily life, but her acceptance removed the fear that she would reject me if I chose both of them.

They entered as she exited, both standing warily in front of me. They eyed me like I was a ticking time bomb about to explode. I supposed that was a reasonable assumption on their part, since I'd stormed out before.

I took a deep breath and tried to quell some of my anger. "Look, I know you guys don't understand why it was so upsetting to me to have the offer of a contract to be your sub, so let me explain it. It's probably a fine proposal for someone who is a submissive and doesn't want more than that. I can't be *just* your sub. I care too much about both of you."

"What is it you want?" asked Dante.

I cocked a brow. "I guess I want everything. When I first went from just dreaming about you to being with you, I convinced myself I could keep things strictly physical and away from the other parts of my life. I was dumb enough to think I could sleep with you, get dumped by you, and probably even stay working as your part-time nanny. I was a bit naïve."

Patrick winced. "Are you quitting?"

I hesitated and then shrugged. "I don't really want to, but I don't see how this can work. I want something neither one of you are prepared to give, and if I keep working for you, I'm just going to end up back in bed with you again. Then I'll love you even more, and I'll be even more shattered when everything finally falls apart. I have to get out now, while I can still handle breaking up." Maybe I could handle it. I was certain there would be lots of sleepless nights, tears, and pints of Häagen-Dazs in my future.

Dante took a step forward. "I'm not going to accept your resignation. Instead, I'd like to promote you."

I rolled my eyes. "How the fuck does that help anything? It still doesn't solve the personal problems between us."

They both seemed surprised that I had cursed, but then shared an amused look.

"It's another position Dante has in mind, and you'd be perfect for it."

I gave Patrick a skeptical look. "What is it? *Uncontracted* submissive?" I asked with biting sarcasm.

"Our wife," they both said in unison.

I blinked, certain I had misheard for a moment. "Your wife?" I shook my head. "You don't really mean it. It's just a ploy to get me back until you're done with me."

Dante looked angry. "We don't say things we don't mean, and we'd never lie about such a thing."

"If you think we'd trick you into being our sub by pretending to want to marry you, you don't know us at all." Patrick sounded wounded.

I sighed and ran a hand through my still-messy hair. I hadn't yet had a chance to brush it since I'd run from their home. "I don't really think you'd do that. I guess it was just a knee-jerk reaction. It's just so unbelievable that you're proposing. Are you really serious?"

As one, they both dropped to one knee and looked up at me. "We don't have an engagement ring," said Patrick.

"But we can get one," added Dante.

"If this is what you need to be happy, and what you want from us, it's what we want to give you. We genuinely want a future with you, Jessa."

I blinked at Patrick's words and held out my hands, taking the ones they held up. When they both stood up and curved their arms around me, I knew they were sincere. They genuinely wanted me to be with them forever, and they were willing to risk their hearts in the process. I could do no less. "Yes, I'll marry you."

Chapter Eleven

Jessa

Our wedding consisted of a private ceremony between the three of us in a rented log cabin at high enough elevations to still have snow on the ground in April. The children are with Patrick's parents for the weekend, and they were in safe hands. I adored his family, who'd opened their arms and hearts to me.

According to Dante, Victoria—being a decade older and seemingly too far out of their leagues—had faced a slightly cooler reception until the Shelleys became convinced a triad was the kind of relationship Patrick and Dante wanted, and that Victoria wasn't taking advantage of them or targeting them for money.

I benefited from Victoria having opened their minds to the possibility. I also benefited from her having taught my husbands how to love, and how to dominate. They were quite good at it, and I was getting good at submitting. We were happy.

We had exchanged matching rings earlier in the night, and they had also given me a set of earrings to match the huge diamond in my engagement ring as well. There was still one gift I hadn't given them yet, but I planned to do so tonight. They hadn't pushed me or asked about it, and I was certain they were leaving it up to me if or when I was ready for both of them.

I left the bathroom with damp hair pinned up on my head, my body slathered with vanilla-scented lotion, and not a stitch of clothing.

They waited for me in the giant king-size bed, and there was a space right between them reserved just for me. I was sidetracked momentarily from my seduction as I remembered Tam and Sam's response the first time they had found us all sleeping together. They'd been so nonchalant about it, as though it was no big deal. They'd been more excited to find out we were going out for breakfast than they were that I was moving in. They hadn't objected to my change in status and seemed happy to have me there, so it had been a good reaction.

"You're absolutely exquisite," said Dante.

"Your extravagant praise is unnecessary, but appreciated." I winked at him as I sashayed forward, putting a deliberate sway in my hips that made both of them moan.

I took my rightful place between them, and they both turned toward me. Patrick started kissing my neck, and my lips moved with Dante's as we kissed like we had never kissed before. It was like that every time, and I was certain that part of our relationship would never change. I was going to love and desire both of them until the day I died, and I knew it was the same for them.

Hands moved over me, coaxing and caressing me into a fevered state. Mine were just as busy, as was my mouth. I teased Patrick, sucking until he was near coming before pulling away to turn my attention to Dante.

He held up his cock, clearly expecting my mouth to encompass it, but I just grinned at him as I chose to straddle him instead. He slid his cockhead down my slit until finding the opening of my pussy and eased inside me. This time, there were no barriers between us as we'd all made the decision to throw away contraceptive and try to add to the family.

Patrick groaned behind me. "It's unfair to leave a guy hanging like this."

I grinned at him. "Maybe I can make it up to you."

He arched a brow. "What did you have in mind?"

I took a deep breath. "I'm ready for both of you."

"You mean...?" Dante trailed off.

I nodded as Patrick let out a sound of excitement.

"We'll go slowly and carefully."

I nodded at Dante's reassurance, but I wasn't terrified about was coming. Much like I had prepared for Patrick to claim my ass for the first time with ever-larger plugs, I had been using dildos to prepare myself for this as well.

Patrick lubed himself well before squirting more inside me to cover my insides and Dante's cock, already firmly buried in my sheath.

At first, I was sure the amount of lube was excessive, but as Patrick guided his dick inside me on top of Dante's, pressing slowly and carefully to open me beyond anything I'd experienced before, I was relieved he'd used so much. It hurt, but two cocks inside my pussy also created a delicious friction that was quickly overtaking any discomfort.

It was a good thing I'd been working up to this, because there was no way I could've taken them both at the same time without some preparation. My husbands were too large to make it feasible. The idea of having done so as a virgin was laughable, so I was glad they hadn't tried that our first time together.

It seemed to take forever before Patrick was deeply inside me, and then they started to thrust slowly. They moved in opposing rhythm, so there was always a cock deeper inside me while the other one was withdrawing. Neither one left me completely though, and I was soon just as eager as they were.

It was amazing, though I'd never expected to truly enjoy it. I'd figured it would be something I would do for them upon occasion because I loved them, not because I liked it—but that was the farthest thing from the truth. I had been naïve about that as well. I loved having both of their shafts inside me, and there was an amazing closeness between the three of us. I'd certainly picked the right time to try this, as it was the perfect seal on our unofficial marriage.

When the three of us came together at the same time, I wasn't surprised. We were often in sync like that, but it was still far more intense than ever before. Perhaps it was partly because we were joined without condoms, and I could feel their mingled cum settling inside me, but I knew it was more than that. This act bonded us on an entirely new level, and further strengthened our relationship, while reminding me and them of our shared love.

Epilogue

Jessa

Our home was packed with family and friends who'd gathered for Danny's celebration party. Now that he was a few weeks old and ready to be admired, the party was to welcome him into our world.

And he'd taken our world by storm. He came in the middle of the night, and he had the same black curls as Dante and Cori, but my blue eyes. Every time I looked at him, I fell in love all over again with my tiny son. It was the same for both of my husbands and our kids, and now for our extended family.

They'd been passing Danny around for more than an hour at this point, and I was getting impatient to hold him again. It couldn't be much longer before he'd want to eat, so I could escape and have a few minutes alone with Danny while nursing him.

Unless Patrick or Dante decided to come in, or the twins or Cori wanted to keep me company. That was unlikely today, since they were occupied with cousins and children of friends at the party, but it wasn't uncommon. They were equally fascinated with Danny as the rest of us were, and I was glad to see the bond between the siblings. At seven weeks, Danny didn't yet recognize how lucky he was to have so much love surrounding him, but I knew. I knew and was grateful for it every day.

My mom had finally managed to wrest Danny from great-aunt Dinah, and she was clearly enamored too. She'd been like that ever since she first held him in the hospital. She had lived up to her promise and supported us in everything. Fortunately, she'd also quickly grown to like Dante and Patrick, so there was little reason for her not to approve or support our relationship. They treated her with respect, and she did the same for all of us.

The Shelleys were equally generous and openminded, and we truly were one big, happy family. Having grown up the only child of a single mother, with no idea of my dad's whereabouts, it was like a dream come true. If there was some design in the universe, where Fate had planned out my life, she must have recognized I needed more love than some people, so she had given me two husbands.

I didn't really believe in such a concept, but I liked to imagine sometimes that somewhere in the universe, someone had designated Patrick and Dante just for me. Knowing it was far more likely that a random series of events had brought us all together made it all the more amazing that we had found each other. I intended to cling to what we'd found for the rest of my life, and I was confident they felt the same way.